OAK TREE TALES

Miss Mouse Takes a Holiday

Dorothea King

Miss Mouse had only just got up, and was about to have her early morning cup of tea when there was a loud knock at the door.

"Who can that be?" she said, glancing at the clock. "No-one visits at this time of the morning."

On the doorstep was the postman with an Express Delivery letter.

"You'll have to sign for it," he said, thrusting the letter into her hand.

Miss Mouse had never received an important letter before and couldn't wait to open it.

"Probably bad news," the postman said grimly. "They usually are."

Miss Mouse ignored him and shut the door, he was always grumpy, especially when the sun was shining.

Miss Mouse poured herself a cup of tea and started to read her letter.

It was from her cousin Alice whom she hadn't seen for at least four years. The letter was very brief and to the point:

> Have to go and look after my sick mother.
> Husband away. Please come and take care
> of the children. It will be a holiday for you
> — Love Alice.

"Well, that's not bad news," said Miss Mouse delightedly. "From what I can remember she has two sweet little children."

When she had finished her tea Miss Mouse quickly dressed and went around to Mistress Hedgehog's house. Not knowing exactly how long she would be away, she would have to make arrangements for someone to look after her house.

Mistress Hedgehog was most obliging and said she would do all she could to help. "After all, that's what friends are for, my dear."

DO NOT DISTURB

Miss Mouse was on her way back home when she met Master Rabbit who, having nothing better to do, wanted to stop and chat.

"I really can't stop," said Miss Mouse, and explained why she was in such a hurry. The rabbit was most helpful and said that he would escort her some of the way.

"In fact, I could push you on my barrow," he said.

Knowing the kind of mishaps which occured when the rabbit was around, Miss Mouse declined the invitation, but said she would be most obliged if he would carry her case.

"Case? Who is going away?" said a voice from above.

Sir Squirrel strode into the clearing. He was obviously on his way to some kind of business meeting as he was wearing a striped suit and carried an important-looking briefcase.

"My dear chap," he said, patting the rabbit on the back. "We'll be sorry to see you go."

"Oh, I'm not going anywhere," said the rabbit. "It's Miss Mouse who's going away."

For some unknown reason Sir Squirrel looked slightly disappointed and muttered, "Oh well, better luck next time," as he strolled off down the woodland path.

All that day Miss Mouse made preparations for leaving the house. There was a great deal to do. She cleaned every room from top to bottom, watered the pot-plants, put a note out for the milkman, cancelled the morning papers and, last of all, packed her case.

Before she left the following morning she gave Mistress Hedgehog her key, and, after a brief farewell, set off, with the rabbit carrying her case.

"Be sure to write," called Mistress Hedgehog.

The rabbit went as far as the edge of the wood, which was roughly halfway, and then Miss Mouse thanked him for his help and continued on her way.

It was almost sunset by the time she reached the meadow where her cousin lived. It was a very pretty meadow, with lots of buttercups, daisies and sweet-smelling clover. Through the middle ran a small stream which Miss Mouse remembered she must cross to get to her cousin's house on the other side.

"I had quite forgotten how pretty it is," she said as she caught sight of the house.

It was built low in a bank, surrounded by wild roses, honeysuckle and clumps of moss.

Gently she knocked on the door which was opened almost immediately by a pretty mouse holding a baby.

"My dear Miss Mouse, how lovely to see you," said her cousin Alice. "Do come in."

After they had exchanged greetings Alice went to make a welcome cup of tea while Miss Mouse held the baby.

"He's so sweet," she cooed. "I expect your other children are quite grown-up by now."

"Oh yes," called Alice from the kitchen. "They can be quite a handful sometimes."

She came back carrying a tray, and then put the baby in the crib while they drank their tea and caught up on family news.

Afterwards Alice said that as she had to make an early start in the morning perhaps Miss Mouse would like to see 'the others'.

"Thankfully they are sound asleep at the moment," she laughed as she led the way down the corridor.

Miss Mouse didn't quite see how two small children could be so much of a problem. That is until Alice opened the bedroom door.

There weren't *two* children but masses of them.
The entire room was lined with beds, cots, cribs and even hammocks.
"Gosh," gasped Miss Mouse.
"Yes, aren't they lovely?" Alice whispered.

Miss Mouse was so surprised that she could hardly speak. "L-lovely," she agreed in amazement. And tried to count the beds. She had reached ten when Alice hustled her out, and took her back down the corridor to a tiny room where Miss Mouse would sleep.

Miss Mouse was in a complete flurry. What would she *do* with them all. There must be *hundreds* of them in there.

It was with mixed feelings that she went to bed that night, glad of the rest but dreading the day to come.

"My name's Katy," said a voice from the bottom of the bed.

Miss Mouse opened one eye sleepily. Sitting on the end of the bed was a little mouse, eating a slice of toast from which marmalade dripped in large blobs onto the eiderdown.

"Oh dear, the day has begun," Miss Mouse whispered to herself.

Alice went soon after breakfast leaving Miss Mouse with an extremely long list of 'do's and don'ts'.

The first thing she did was to try and learn all of the names of the children, but there were so many of them, and they all appeared to look alike. It seemed to be an impossible task. It was then that Miss Mouse came up with a brilliant idea. She would give them all numbers.

Quickly she cut out lots of pieces of paper and numbered them, explaining to the little mice that they must keep them pinned on their backs, "At all times?"

That first day was a complete disaster. Miss Mouse seemed to spend all her time wiping dirty fingers, changing muddy clothes, preparing meals and washing dishes.

It was an absolute relief when bathtime came and she knew that within an hour they would all be sound asleep. Or would they…?

Apart from getting up in the middle of
the night to give No.2 a drink of water...

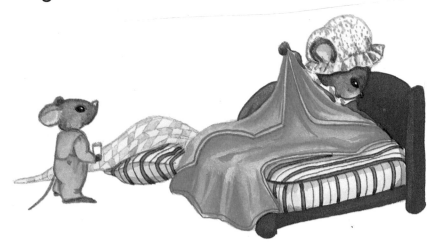

...and then having to change the bed when he spilt it;

cuddling No.10 when he had a
nightmare;

finding a rag-doll which No. 12 had lost
at the bottom of her bed;

reading a quick story to No. 4 because
"Mummy always did."

Apart from all of that it was a peaceful night, and
eventually Miss Mouse *did* get to sleep — and woke up
the following morning feeling completely exhausted.

The day was warm and bright and Miss Mouse decided that she would take them all on a picnic. The children thought this was a wonderful idea, and even suggested where they might go.

"It's got a place where we can paddle," said No. 6.

"And there's lots of mud," added No. 11 in delight.

"There's hundreds and hundreds of hiding places," yelled No. 10.

"You got lost last time and Daddy had to spend all night looking for you," No. 3 reminded him.

"But I got stuck," No. 10 argued. "It wasn't my fault."

"You shouldn't have climbed so far up the tree," said No. 9.

"Oh dear," said Miss Mouse, pressing a hand to her head. "Perhaps we should choose somewhere else to have a picnic."

"Oh no. You'll *love* it," they all cried.

Miss Mouse wasn't too sure she agreed but, nevertheless, allowed herself to be led along to the picnic place.

It was indeed a lovely spot, and surprisingly the children played all morning without any disasters occuring.

After an early lunch Miss Mouse began to doze in the sunshine. At first it was only a little doze, but, as the afternoon wore on and the sun grew warmer, she drifted into a deep sleep. After all she *had* lost such a lot of sleep the night before.

It was the night air which woke her. Sleepily she opened her eyes and shivered — it was cold, dark and very, very quiet. Suddenly Miss Mouse leapt to her feet and looked around frantically. There wasn't a child in sight.

Hour after hour she went up and down the meadow calling out their numbers, but there was no reply. The children had gone. Miss Mouse was horrified. What could she do? Where could she look?

At last she could look no further and shaking with fear and exhaustion she stumbled back to the house.

"SURPRISE! SURPRISE!" they all yelled as she flung open the kitchen door.

Miss Mouse looked at them in a stunned silence. The table was laid for tea, the kettle hissed on the hob — and every single one of the children was there, safe and sound.

"Come and sit down," said No. 10, pulling out a chair. "We've made you a lovely tea of ice cream and sausages."

"I couldn't eat a single thing," said Miss Mouse weakly as she fell into the chair.

The following morning Miss Mouse sent a telegram by Pigeon Post. It was addressed to Mistress Hedgehog and contained one word:

HELP!

Mistress Hedgehog arrived late that night and immediately took charge of the situation. The very first thing she did was to send Miss Mouse to bed.

"You look as if you could do with a holiday, my dear," she laughed.

The rest of the week went by like clockwork. Mistress Hedgehog divided all the children into teams and they were each given a chore to do every day.

Meals were eaten in three sittings and everyone washed up their own plates.

Every afternoon they were taken for a walk ...

and then allowed to play.

Bathtime was precisely at half past six ...

followed by a story and then bed.

On Saturday morning Alice arrived home to find the house spick and span, lunch almost ready and the children playing peacefully in the garden.

She was most grateful to Miss Mouse and Mistress Hedgehog.

"I suppose you wouldn't like another holiday next year?" she asked Miss Mouse.

"Only if I can bring a friend," laughed Miss Mouse.